THE SONG OF THE CAMPFIRE

THE SONG OF THE CAMPFIRE

by ROBERT SERVICE

Illustrated by
RICHARD GALABURR

DODD, MEAD & COMPANY

NEW YORK

Text copyright 1912 by Dodd, Mead & Company, Inc.
Copyright renewed 1939 by Robert Service
Illustrations copyright © 1978 by Richard Galaburr
All rights reserved. No part of this book may be reproduced in any form
without permission in writing from the publisher.
Printed in the United States of America.

1 2 3 4 5 6 7 8 9 10

Library of Congress Cataloging in Publication Data

Service, Robert William, 1874–1958.
The song of the campfire.

I. Title.
PR6037.E72S45   1978   811'.5'2   78-15108
ISBN 0-396-07623-8

ESPÉRANCE

*Illustrations of impressions created by verse may seem un-
necessary to some. Nevertheless, I believe many who admire
the work of Robert Service will welcome visual images for
this enlightening poem. The illustrations are inspired by
Mr. Service's insight, and I hope that the reader will see in
them a spark of the illuminating source.*

R.G.

LIST OF ILLUSTRATIONS

THE SONG OF THE CAMPFIRE

Part I

HEED me, feed me, I am hungry, I am red-tongued with desire;
Boughs of balsam, slabs of cedar, gummy fagots of the pine,
Heap them on me, let me hug them to my eager heart of fire,
Roaring, soaring up to heaven as a symbol and a sign.

Bring me knots of sunny maple, silver birch and tamarack;
Leaping, sweeping, I will lap them with my ardent wings of
      flame;
I will kindle them to glory, I will beat the darkness back;
Streaming, gleaming, I will goad them to my glory and my fame.

Bring me gnarly limbs of live-oak, aid me in my frenzied fight;
Strips of iron-wood, scaly blue-gum, writhing redly in my hold;
With my lunge of lurid lances, with my whips that flail the
      night,
They will burgeon into beauty, they will foliate in gold.

Let me star the dim sierras, stab with light the inland seas;
Roaming wind and roaring darkness! seek no mercy at my
      hands;
I will mock the marly heavens, lamp the purple prairies,
I will flaunt my deathless banners down the far, unhouseled
      lands.

In the vast and vaulted pine-gloom where the pillared forests
    frown,
By the sullen, bestial rivers running where God only knows,
On the starlit coral beaches when the combers thunder down,
In the death-spell of the barrens, in the shudder of the snows.

In a blazing belt of triumph from the palm-leaf to the pine,
As a symbol of defiance lo! the wilderness I span;
And my beacons burn exultant as an everlasting sign
Of unending domination of the mastery of Man.

I, the Life, the fierce Uplifter, I that weaned him from the
    mire;
I, the angel and the devil; I, the tyrant and the slave;
I, the Spirit of the Struggle; I, the mighty God of Fire;
I, the Maker and Destroyer; I, the Giver and the Grave.

Part 2

Gather round me, boy and grey-beard, frontiersman of every
    kind.
Few are you, and far and lonely, yet an army forms behind:
By your camp-fires shall they know you, ashes scattered to the
    wind.

Peer into my heart of solace, break your bannock at my blaze;
Smoking, stretched in lazy shelter, build your castles as you
    gaze;
Or, it may be, deep in dreaming, think of dim, unhappy days.

Let my warmth and glow caress you, for your trails are grim and
    hard;
Let my arms of comfort press you, hunger-hewn and battle-
    scarred;
O my lovers! how I bless you with your lives so madly marred!

For you seek the silent spaces, and their secret lore you glean;
For you win the savage races, and the brutish Wild you wean;
And I gladden desert places, where camp-fire has never been.

From the Pole unto the Tropics is there trail ye have not dared?
And because you hold death lightly, so by death shall you be
      spared,
(As the sages of the ages in their pages have declared.)

On the roaring Arkilinik in a leaky bark canoe;
Up the cloud of Mount McKinley, where the avalanche leaps
      through;
In the furnace of Death Valley, when the mirage glimmers blue.

Now a smudge of wiry willows on the weary Kuskoquim;
Now a flare of gummy pine-knots where Vancouver's scaur is
      grim;
Now a gleam of sunny ceiba, when the Cuban beaches dim.

Always, always God's Great Open: lo! I burn with keener light
In the corridors of silence, in the vestibules of night;
'Mid the ferns and grasses gleaming, was there ever gem so
      bright?

Not for weaklings, not for women, like my brother of the
      hearth;
Ring your songs of wrath around me, I was made for manful
      mirth,
In the lusty, gusty greatness, on the bald spots of the earth.

Men, my masters! men, my lovers! ye have fought and ye have
      bled;
Gather round my ruddy embers, softly glowing is my bed;
By my heart of solace dreaming, rest ye and be comforted!

I am dying, O my masters! by my fitful flame ye sleep;
    My purple plumes of glory droop forlorn.
Grey ashes choke and cloak me, and above the pines there creep
    The stealthy silver moccasins of morn.

There comes a countless army, it's the Legion of the Light;
    It tramps in gleaming triumph round the world;
And before its jewelled lances all the shadows of the night
    Back in to abysmal darknesses are hurled.

Leap to life again, my lovers! ye must toil and never tire;
    The day of daring, doing, brightens clear,
When the bed of spicy cedar and the jovial camp-fire
    Must only be a memory of cheer.

There is hope and golden promise in the vast portentous dawn;
    There is glamour in the glad, effluent sky:
Go and leave me; I will dream of you and love you when you're
        gone;
    I have served you, O my masters! let me die.

A little heap of ashes, grey and sodden by the rain,
  Wind-scattered, blurred and blotted by the snow:
Let that be all to tell of me, and glorious again,
  Ye things of greening gladness, leap and glow!

A black scar in the sunshine by the palm-leaf or the pine,
  Blind to the night and dead to all desire;
Yet oh, of life and uplift what a symbol and a sign!
Yet oh, of power and conquest what a destiny is mine!
A little heap of ashes—Yea! a miracle divine,
  The foot-print of a god, all-radiant Fire.